To Matilda, with love xx
—V.F.

To Caroline, with much love
—A.B.

Text copyright © 2000 by Vivian French
Illustrations copyright © 2000 by Alison Bartlett
First American edition 2001 published by Orchard Books
First published in Great Britain in 2000 by Hodder Children's Books

Published by arrangement with Hodder Children's Books

Orchard Books, A Grolier Company
95 Madison Avenue, New York, NY 10016

Printed in Hong Kong
The text of this book is set in 19 point Goudy. The illustrations are gouache.

1 3 5 7 9 10 8 6 4 2

Library of Congress Cataloging-in-Publication Data
French, Vivian.
Oliver's milk shake / by Vivian French ; illustrated by Alison Bartlett.—lst American ed.
p.   cm.
Summary: Aunt Jen takes Oliver to a farm, buys the special ingredients she needs, and makes him a yummy scrummy fruity frothy icy nicy tip-top tasty dreamy creamy milk shake.
ISBN 0-531-30304-7 (trade only)
[1. Milk shakes—Fiction. 2. Aunts—Fiction. 3. Farms—Fiction.] I. Bartlett, Alison, ill. II. Title.
PZ7.F88917 Ok 2001 [E]—dc21 99-44069

Oliver's Milk Shake

by Vivian French

illustrated by

Alison Bartlett

Orchard Books   New York

Mom woke Oliver at eight o'clock.

"Time to get up!" she said. "Remember you're going out for the day with Aunt Jen and Lily."

"Do I have to?" asked Oliver.

"Yes," said Mom. "I'm going shopping."

"Oh," said Oliver. "Maybe I don't mind going with Aunt Jen."

Aunt Jen bustled in just after nine-thirty.

"My goodness, Oliver," she said. "Orange soda for breakfast? Milk is *much* better for your teeth and bones."

Lily made a face.

"I don't . . ." began Oliver.

"You don't like milk!" Aunt Jen wagged a finger at him. "Just like my Lily. What *you* need is one of my yummy milk shakes."

The clock on the town hall struck ten as Aunt Jen, Lily, and
Oliver drove past.
"Where are we going?" asked Oliver.
"Shopping!" said Aunt Jen.
Lily sighed loudly. Oliver looked horrified.
"But Mom said we were going out for
the day!"
"We are," said Aunt Jen, beaming.
"We're going out shopping for
a yummy scrummy
milk shake."

Oliver was surprised when Aunt Jen parked the car.

"Out you hop!" she said cheerfully.

"But there aren't any stores here," said Oliver. "Only fields."

Aunt Jen nodded. "That's right. We're going to a farm. We're going to buy fresh milk from real cows and fresh fruit.

"Then we'll go home again,
and what'll we do then?"
Oliver looked hopeful.
"Watch a video?"
"No!" said Aunt Jen. "We'll
make a yummy scrummy fruity milk shake!"

"Oh," said Oliver.

Aunt Jen led the way down a path.

"Look, Oliver!" said Lily. "Sheep!"

Oliver climbed onto the fence, and a big woolly sheep looked up. "Baa," it said loudly. "Baaaa!"

Lily giggled. "It's asking you if you want a scritchy scratchy puffy fluffy woolly sweater!"

"No thank you," Oliver said. "Tell it I'm going to have a yummy scrummy fruity frothy milk shake."

Lots of hens were strutting and scratching in the yard.
"Cluck!" they said. "Cluck! Cluck! Cluck!"
"Do you put eggs in milk shakes?" Oliver asked.
"My goodness, no!" said Aunt Jen.
"Oh," said Oliver. "I just wondered."
"No yolky jokey eggs," said Lily. "Not in our yummy
scrummy fruity frothy icy milk shake."

"OINK! OINK!"

Oliver jumped. "What's that?"

Aunt Jen laughed loudly. "Pigs, Oliver. Over there!"

Oliver and Lily ran across the farmyard to the pigpen. "Wow!" said Oliver. "She's huge!"

Lily was counting. "Eight . . . nine . . . ten piglets!"

"And they're drinking their milk like good little piglets," said Aunt Jen.

Oliver and Lily looked at each other. "But they're not drinking yummy scrummy fruity frothy icy nicy milk shakes!"

Lily got tired of watching the piglets.
She peeked in the shed.
"Goats!" she said. Oliver came over to see what
she was looking at. So did Aunt Jen.
"Goat's milk is delicious," Aunt Jen told Oliver.
"Yuck!" said Lily. "I *hate* goat's milk."
"Nonsense, Lily." Aunt Jen frowned.
"You've never even tried it."

Oliver saw the cows first. They were big—much bigger than Oliver.

"There!" said Aunt Jen. "Aren't they wonderful? You stay here and look at them, and I'll go and buy our special creamy milk."

Oliver felt a little anxious. "Can I come with you?" he asked.

"I'm coming too," said Lily.

At the farm stand Aunt Jen
bought a big carton of fresh milk.
"Oliver dear, what's your favorite
fruit?" she asked.

"Blueberries," Oliver said.

"Then we'll buy blueberries for our milk
shake," said Aunt Jen.

Lily nodded. "Our yummy
scrummy fruity frothy icy nicy . . .
what was the next part, Oliver?"

Oliver beamed. "Tip-top tasty!"

"Mom!" Oliver rushed into the kitchen. "We're back! And Aunt Jen is going to make a yummy scrummy fruity frothy icy nicy tip-top tasty *dreamy creamy* milk shake."

"I certainly am," said Aunt Jen. "This young man needs his milk."

She pulled out Mom's blender and poured in the milk and blueberries. Then she chopped up a banana and dropped that in along with a little ice.

WHRRRRRRRRRRRRRRRRRRRRRRR

Mom's blender whizzed and whirred.

"There," said Aunt Jen. "You'll just love this!"

"Mmm," said Oliver, sucking on his straw. "This is scrumptious!"

Oliver finished his milk shake with a loud slurp. "Mom," he said, "can I have one of these tonight instead of my usual milk?"

Aunt Jen stared at him. "But, Oliver," she said, "you don't like milk!"

"Yes I do!" Oliver said indignantly. "I only had orange soda for breakfast today because I put too much milk on my cornflakes and there wasn't any left!"